# SCIENCE BEHIND THE
# BLUE-FOOTED
# BOOBIES

by Alicia Z. Klepeis

pogo

# Ideas for Parents and Teachers

Pogo Books let children practice reading informational text while introducing them to nonfiction features such as headings, labels, sidebars, maps, and diagrams, as well as a table of contents, glossary, and index.

Carefully leveled text with a strong photo match offers early fluent readers the support they need to succeed.

### Before Reading

- "Walk" through the book and point out the various nonfiction features. Ask the student what purpose each feature serves.
- Look at the glossary together. Read and discuss the words.

### Read the Book

- Have the child read the book independently.
- Invite him or her to list questions that arise from reading.

### After Reading

- Discuss the child's questions. Talk about how he or she might find answers to those questions.
- Prompt the child to think more. Ask: Blue-footed boobies are named for their blue feet. Do you know of other animals with a color in their names?

Pogo Books are published by Jump!
5357 Penn Avenue South
Minneapolis, MN 55419
www.jumplibrary.com

Copyright © 2021 Jump!
International copyright reserved in all countries.
No part of this book may be reproduced in any form without written permission from the publisher.

Library of Congress Cataloging-in-Publication Data

Names: Klepeis, Alicia, 1971- author.
Title: Blue-footed boobies / Alicia Z. Klepeis.
Description: Pogo books edition.
Minneapolis, MN: Jump!, Inc., [2021]
Series: Science behind the colors | Includes index.
Audience: Ages 7-10 | Audience: Grades 2-3
Identifiers: LCCN 2019056142 (print)
LCCN 2019056143 (ebook)
ISBN 9781645275749 (library binding)
ISBN 9781645275756 (paperback)
ISBN 9781645275763 (ebook)
Subjects: LCSH: Blue-footed booby–Juvenile literature.
Classification: LCC QL696.P48 K 2021 (print)
LCC QL696.P48 (ebook) | DDC 598.4/3–dc23
LC record available at https://lccn.loc.gov/2019056142
LC ebook record available at https://lccn.loc.gov/2019056143

Editor: Jenna Gleisner
Designer: Molly Ballanger

Photo Credits: Don Mammoser/Shutterstock, cover; Lukas Bischoff Photograph/Shutterstock, 1; Piotr Kalinowski Photos/Shutterstock, 3; Kanokratnok/Shutterstock, 4; Vaclav Sebek/Shutterstock, 5; Maridav/Shutterstock, 6-7; NaturesMomentsuk/Shutterstock, 8-9; Martin Prochazkacz/Shutterstock, 10; BlueOrange Studio/Shutterstock, 11; Minden Pictures/SuperStock, 12-13, 14-15, 17; SL-Photography/Shutterstock, 16; Michael S. Nolan/Alamy, 18-19; Nature Picture Library/Alamy, 20-21; Brian Lasenby/Shutterstock, 23.

Printed in the United States of America at Corporate Graphics in North Mankato, Minnesota.

# TABLE OF CONTENTS

**CHAPTER 1**
**Fast Divers** .................................................... 4

**CHAPTER 2**
**Why So Blue?** ............................................... 10

**CHAPTER 3**
**Flashy Feet** .................................................. 16

**ACTIVITIES & TOOLS**
**Try This!** ...................................................... 22
**Glossary** ...................................................... 23
**Index** ........................................................... 24
**To Learn More** ............................................. 24

# CHAPTER 1
# FAST DIVERS

What bird has bright blue feet and dances to show them off? It is a blue-footed booby!

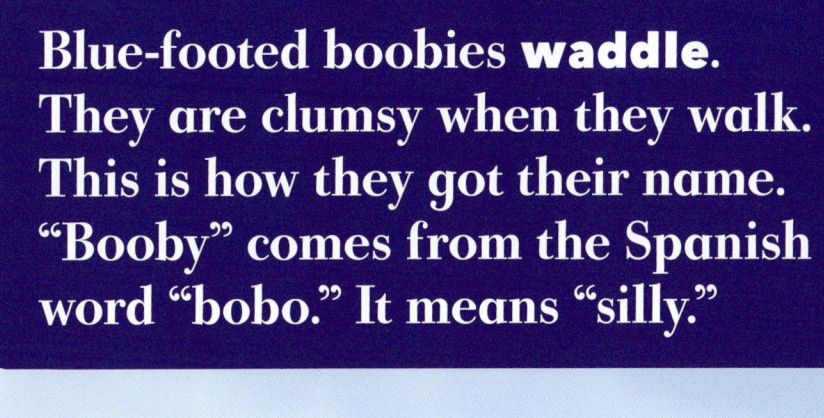

Blue-footed boobies **waddle**. They are clumsy when they walk. This is how they got their name. "Booby" comes from the Spanish word "bobo." It means "silly."

CHAPTER 1　5

Blue-footed boobies are the size of big seagulls. They have long necks and pointed wings. Feathers on their body are white. Feathers on their wings are brown.

### DID YOU KNOW?

Blue-footed booby bills are strong and sharp. They have **serrated** edges. This helps them catch and hold onto fish.

CHAPTER 1   7

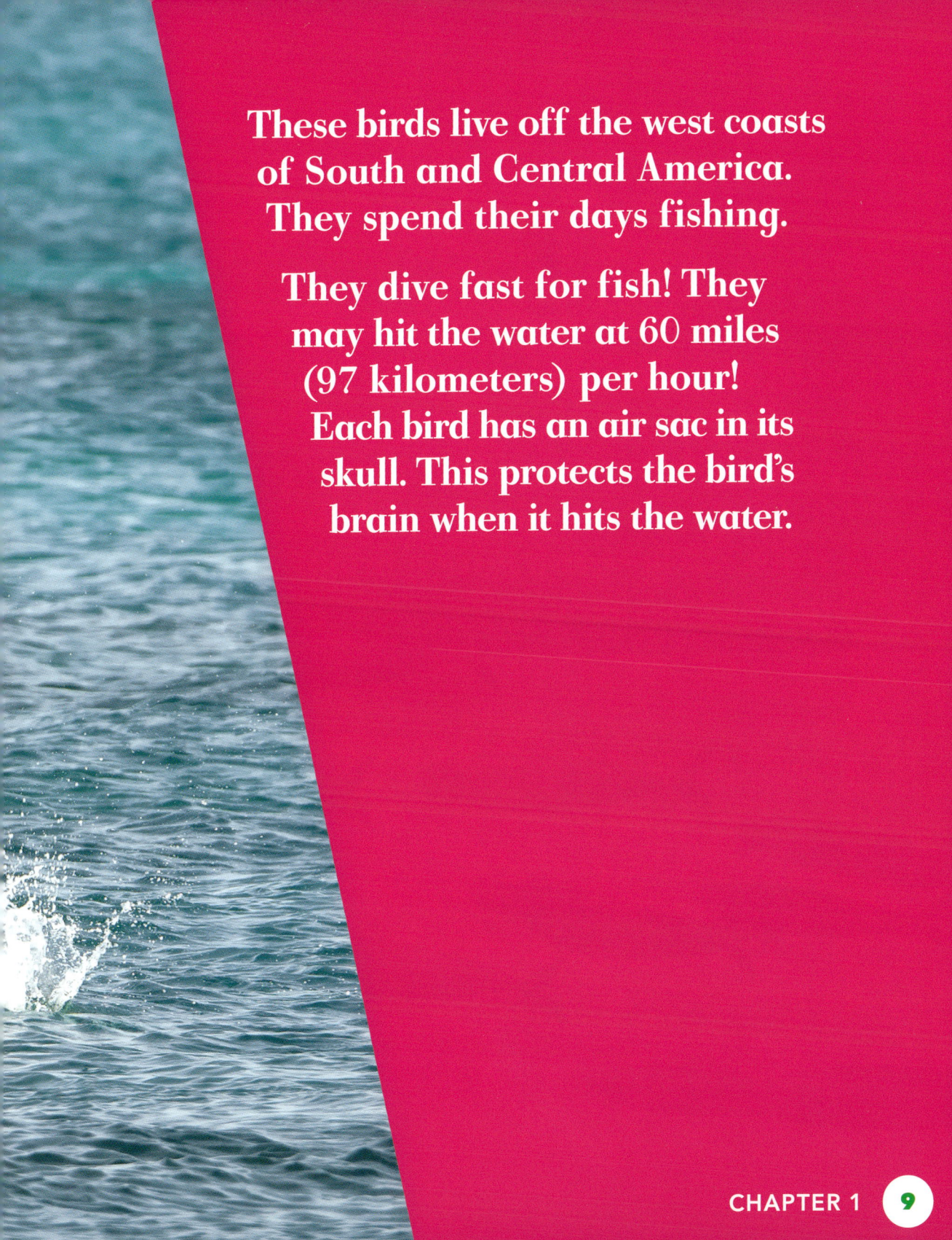

These birds live off the west coasts of South and Central America. They spend their days fishing.

They dive fast for fish! They may hit the water at 60 miles (97 kilometers) per hour! Each bird has an air sac in its skull. This protects the bird's brain when it hits the water.

# CHAPTER 2
# WHY SO BLUE?

So what makes their feet blue? One cause is **collagen** in their skin. It makes their feet look blue. The other cause is the food they eat. Boobies eat fish, such as sardines. These fish have a bright yellow **pigment** in them.

sardines

The yellow from the fish mixes with the blue in their skin. It makes fun-colored feet!

CHAPTER 2

If a blue-footed booby does not eat, the blue changes. After 48 hours without food, the feet turn a darker blue. Once the bird eats again, the color gets brighter. Bright turquoise feet mean the bird is getting enough fish to eat!

## DID YOU KNOW?

Female blue-footed boobies' feet are darker. Why? Their bodies likely put some yellow pigment into their eggs. It does not all go into their feet.

young booby

Not all booby feet are blue. Young boobies have brown feet. They will turn blue when the booby is around two years old. This is when the bird is old enough to **mate**.

CHAPTER 2

# CHAPTER 3
## FLASHY FEET

An adult male flashes his blue feet. Why? It helps him find a mate! He lifts one foot at a time.

The female looks at his feet. The brighter the feet, the more **attractive** she finds him. Why? It means he is healthy and strong. He will be able to give their **offspring** more food. The male bows. He spreads his wings.

CHAPTER 3

The male is proud of his bright blue feet. He keeps showing them off. He gives a gift, too! Perhaps a stone or a twig will **impress** her. She dances back!

# TAKE A LOOK!

There are steps to the mating dance. The male flashes his feet. See what else he does!

① The male lifts one foot at a time.

② He spreads his wings wide. He bows.

③ He points his bill to the sky. He whistles.

④ He clacks his bill with the female's.

⑤ He offers the female a gift.

CHAPTER 3 | 19

If the dance goes well, the pair might mate for life. Boobies nest on land. Both parents care for the chicks. When they're old enough, they will dance, too!

> **DID YOU KNOW?**
>
> Chicks raised by brighter-footed dads grow faster than those with duller feet. Why? These dads pass on excellent **genes** to their offspring. They are good hunters and feed their young well.

20 CHAPTER 3

chick

# ACTIVITIES & TOOLS

## TRY THIS!

### CHANGING COLOR

Blue-footed boobies' feet change color according to what they eat. See how color moves through something with this activity!

**What You Need:**
- measuring cup
- water
- glass
- teaspoon
- blue or red food coloring
- knife
- ruler
- one stalk of celery (keep the leaves on)
- pencil
- notebook

1. Pour about ¾ cup (180 milliliters) of water into the glass.
2. Add 2½ teaspoons (12 mL) of food coloring to the water. Stir until mixed well.
3. Ask an adult to cut off the bottom 1½ inches (4 centimeters) from a stalk of celery.
4. Put the celery in the water with the cut end facing down.
5. Leave the celery in the colored water overnight.
6. What happened to the celery? Record your results in your notebook.

# GLOSSARY

**attractive:** Enjoyable to look at or experience.

**collagen:** A kind of protein in the skin and tissue of animals.

**genes:** Parts of living things that are passed from parents to offspring and determine how one looks and grows.

**impress:** To make someone or something feel admiration or respect.

**mate:** To join together to produce babies.

**offspring:** The young of animals, people, or plants.

**pigment:** A substance that gives color to something.

**serrated:** Having a jagged, saw-like edge.

**waddle:** To walk awkwardly, taking short steps and moving slightly from side to side.

ACTIVITIES & TOOLS    23

# INDEX

air sac 9
bills 6, 19
bows 17, 19
Central America 9
chicks 20
collagen 10
dances 4, 18, 19, 20
dive 9
eat 10, 12
eggs 12
feathers 6
feet 4, 10, 11, 12, 15, 16, 17, 18, 19, 20
female 12, 17, 18, 19
fish 6, 9, 10, 11, 12
genes 20
male 16, 17, 18, 19
mate 15, 16, 20
necks 6
nest 20
offspring 17, 20
pigment 10, 12
size 6
South America 9
waddle 5
wings 6, 17, 19
young 15, 20

# TO LEARN MORE

Finding more information is as easy as 1, 2, 3.

❶ Go to www.factsurfer.com
❷ Enter "blue-footedboobies" into the search box.
❸ Click the "Surf" button to see a list of websites.

24 ACTIVITIES & TOOLS